The Mary D and the Turtle

Anne Worrall and Tanya Banks • Illustrated by David Webster

Really Good Books

Welcome to the little
seaside village of
Port Isaac in Cornwall.

This is where Will, his dad,
Fisherman Jack and his
dog, Connie all live.

How many seagulls can you see?
(Answer on page 31)

"Ah, peace at last!
Just you and me and the sea, eh Will?"
sighed Fisherman Jack.

He lay back and closed his eyes.

"Dad, dad! I think I've caught something!"
shouted Will in excitement, as his rod bent over.

"Oh no! Just look at that, Dad! Why do people throw plastic rubbish like this into the sea?" asked Will angrily.

"Don't they realise what harm all this stuff does to the creatures that live in the sea?"

"They either don't realise or they don't care,"

replied his dad.

"We'd better keep the sun off these fish, if we want them to be fresh for tonight's barbecue."

"If people saw all the rubbish we see far out at sea, they'd realise how bad it is,"

declared Will, his mouth full of sandwich.

"Come over here and look at this, Will,"
said his dad excitedly.

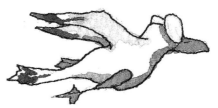

"Seals!

*Look, they've got pups and
they're coming this way!"*

"This one's got a tag on its back flipper," Will pointed out to his dad.

"This tag's got a number, Dad.
That means she's been rescued by the Seal Sanctuary.

They'll be pleased to know
she's doing well," said Will
and wrote the number on
the back of his hand.

"Oh no!" cried Will.

"There's a plastic bag in the water. The pups are going to get tangled up in it. I 'll grab hold of it."

In his hurry to save the pups, Will leaned too far out and lost his balance.

"Aagh! Help!"

Just in time Fisherman
Jack grabbed Will
and pulled him back
on board.

" *Don't worry,*
Will, I'll take care of the bag, " he said.

He leaned over the side and
caught hold of the bag.

" *Ouch!* "

yelled Fisherman Jack,

" *It's a jellyfish and it's stung me!* "

His hand began to swell.

"Ow! This really hurts. I think we'd better head for home. Will, can you take the wheel?"

Will steered the Mary D safely back into the harbour and then helped his dad into the dinghy.

Fisherman Jack's hand was so painful, he couldn't hold the oars.

Will rowed the dinghy safely back to shore.

Then Will remembered that they had left the tub of fish on board the Mary D.

"I'll go back, Dad," he said.

"No, Will," replied his dad.
"We'll leave the fish for the seagulls. Let's go home."

"Not without our fish for the barbecue," declared Will, and he set off back to the Mary D.

Suddenly the dinghy lurched to one side. It had hit something under the water.

One of the oars fell into the sea. Will looked down and saw a big, dark shape below the waves.

"Oh no!" he cried, *"Whatever's that?"*

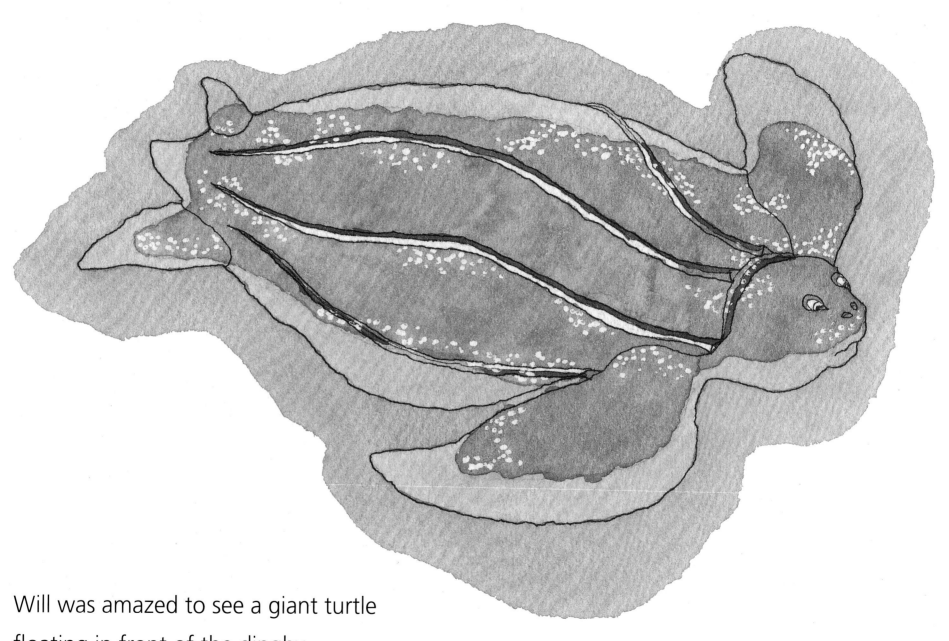

Will was amazed to see a giant turtle
floating in front of the dinghy.

He leaned over the side to try to grab his oar, but the dinghy
tipped over and Will fell into the deep, dark water.

"*Help!*" he shouted.

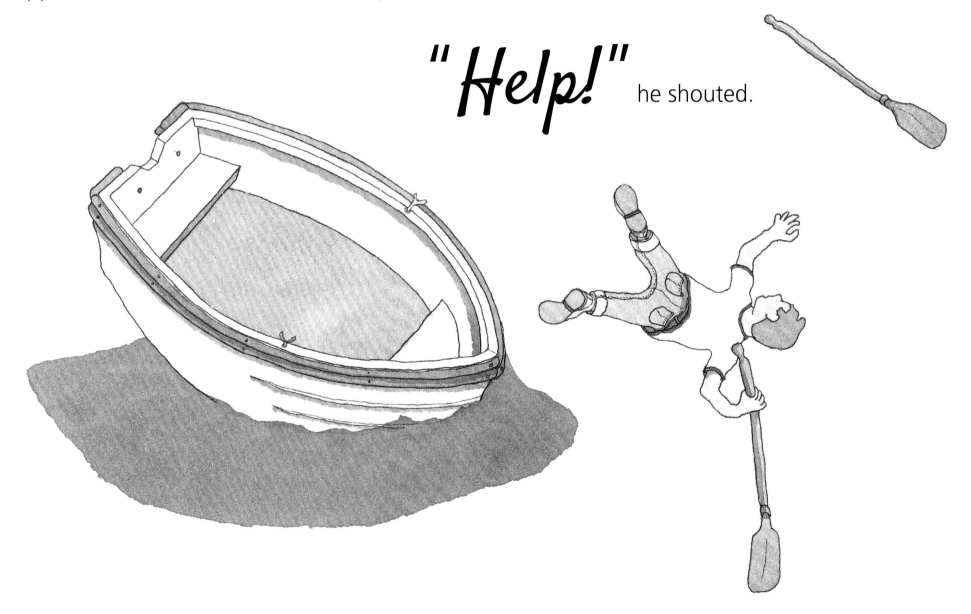

Will tried to swim but his heavy boots were dragging him down under the water. He began to panic.

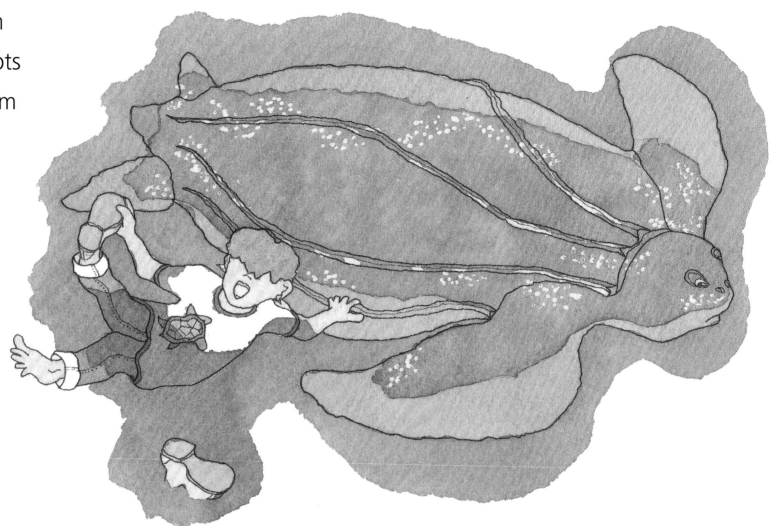

The turtle looked at Will then swam slowly over to his side. Will was able to hold on to the turtle's shell, as he struggled to pull off his boots.

Will, no longer scared, hugged the turtle.
"*Oh, thank you, thank you!*" he gasped.

He gazed at her in wonder.
"*I've never seen a turtle as big and beautiful as you.*"

Will heard the sound of a boat's engine in the distance.
"Look, that must be the Wavehunters' boat
coming back from their day out," Will told the turtle.
"I hope they can see us,"

"Hey!
Over here!
Help!"

he shouted and
waved madly.

Andy, the skipper soon pulled Will to safety on board his boat.

Andy then examined the turtle who was now hardly moving.

"She's a leatherback, something
you hardly ever see round here,"
he explained,

wavehunters

" But she's what we call a
'bubble butt'. She's eaten plastic
and her stomach 's full of gas.
This makes her float. She can't
dive and before long she'll
starve to death."

Back on shore Will told his dad,
"The turtle saved my life.
We can't let her die!"

Andy was ringing
the Sealife Centre.

"Well, we've done all
we can," he told Will.

"Divers are on their way. They'll
take her to the Sealife Sanctuary
to see if they can save her."

Later that evening Fisherman Jack had a phonecall.

"All's well, " he told Will, "your turtle is at the Sanctuary. They say they can remove the plastic from her stomach and she'll be back swimming around in the sea very soon!"

"Great!" yelled Will. "But we have to get rid of all that plastic in the sea," he declared forcefully. "You're right," agreed his dad, "We must all do our bit to make the seas safe for the creatures who live there."

It had been another big adventure for a little boat.

The Cornish Seal Sanctuary

The Cornish Seal Sanctuary rescues and looks after marine animals of all kinds who have been injured or become separated from their mums. Each season the Sanctuary rescues and nurses over 70 seal pups, until they are ready to go back into the sea.

The Sanctuary also provides a permanent home for animals that need special care from their team of marine animal experts.

Hello my name is Uno

The seal that features in our story is a real seal called Uno.

She was rescued by the Sanctuary when she was abandoned by her mum as a pup. Uno has been seen and reported several times off the North Cornish coast.

Leatherback Turtles

Leatherbacks are the largest turtles in the world and can grow to over 2 metres long and weigh up to 900kg.
That is heavier than ten men!

These turtles live mainly on jellyfish. This means they are at great risk of swallowing by mistake some of the many plastic bags that float around in the sea. They often die as a result of this.